RUBBED OUT

Rob Childs
Illustrated by Philip Trenerry

In the Market

... where nine-year-old Marcus, a keen artist, can't resist a brightly-patterned rubber. He just has to have it – at any cost ...

"How much?"

"Too much for you, little boy."

Marcus pulled a face at the old woman and put the diamond-shaped rubber back down on the stall. He loved its red zigzag lines, which looked like rows of sharp, bloodstained teeth. He really wanted a rubber like that.

"I've got all my pocket money," he told her.

"Not enough," she snapped. "Go away."

He did go away, but not very far. Marcus pretended to look round the other stalls in the Sunday market, but they held no interest for him. He kept wandering back past the old woman's display of bric-a-brac.

"You again!" she snorted. "What do you want?"

"That rubber."

"It ain't meant for the likes o' you, little boy," she said.

"Why not? I'm good at drawing – look."

Marcus held up his sketchbook and flipped over some of the pages.

"Well if you're so good, you don't need to use no rubber," she told him. "Now scram."

Marcus sighed and moved off. He went to sit on the base of a statue in the market square, opened the sketchbook and tugged a pencil out of his coat pocket.

He began to draw the rubber from memory, recreating its patterns perfectly. The rubber looked so real, it almost seemed as if he could lift it from the page.

Then he started work on a cartoon-style sketch of the old woman. He made her look like a witch with a long nose and pointed hat, her black cloak blowing in the wind as she flew on a broomstick.

Marcus decided to go and show her the picture – from a safe distance. He walked back into the market and called out to gain her attention.

"Hey! Look at this."

She peered his way and scowled. "What's that, little boy?"

"You!" he cried.

Acting upon a sudden impulse, he darted forward to the stall, grabbed the rubber and ran off before she could do anything to stop him.

With the woman's screams of rage still echoing in his ears, Marcus kept running until he reached the park. He felt sure he'd be safe there, well away from the market. He sat on a bench near the lake to examine the rubber more closely. Its jagged patterns looked even brighter now, seeming to reflect the sunlight.

"It's wicked!" he exclaimed. "Can't wait to show it around at school."

Marcus gave little thought as to why he had stolen the rubber. He'd never done such a thing before, but he didn't let the theft bother him.

"It's mine now," he grinned, turning the rubber over and over in his hand. "Serves the old witch right. Let's try it out on her. See if it's as good as it looks."

As Marcus began to erase the witch picture, a dizzy feeling swept over him and he closed his eyes for a few moments to let it pass. He had no idea that the woman herself was creeping up behind him across the grass ...

10

In the Park

... where Marcus discovers the special powers of the rubber ...

"Got you!"

Those were the old woman's last words. She made other noises, but they were just splutters and gasps as Marcus whirled round in alarm. He was just in time to catch sight of her fading form before she vanished from view.

Marcus jumped to his feet in alarm, jerking the sketchbook and rubber onto the grass.

"Where are you?" he cried.

There was no sign of the market trader and Marcus had to sit down again on the bench. His legs were shaking so much, they could barely hold him up.

He leant forward to pick up the rubber and stared at the blank page of the book. There was not even a smudge mark on the paper.

"I just don't understand it," he said to himself. "She totally disappeared. Perhaps she really *was* a witch ..."

Marcus sought comfort in his sketching, as he often did when feeling troubled. He doodled at first. Then he noticed a duck that was swimming on the lake and started to draw it.

"Don't go away, little ducky," he said under his breath, glancing up occasionally as his pencil brought the duck to life on the page.

He liked drawing animals and had done many pictures of Jinks, the family tabby cat. This time, perhaps because of being upset, he couldn't get the shape quite right, at least not to his satisfaction.

Normally, he would just alter the sketch, using shading, or even start a new drawing – but now he rubbed the duck out instead.

"Might as well, I guess. The rubber's so clean."

After he had erased the sketch – and recovered from another short dizzy spell – he looked again for the duck, but it was nowhere to be seen.

"Funny – that's gone as well."

Marcus assumed that it must have flown off or rejoined the other ducks on the grass, but then he began to link the two disappearances with the rubber.

"It can't do that, surely," he murmured, looking at the rubber almost in awe. "Perhaps that's why the old woman didn't want me to have it."

He put his idea to the test by drawing the bench. When he had finished, he rubbed it out, and suddenly found himself sitting on the wet grass, his head spinning. The bench had gone.

"Wow!" he gasped. "This is just – *incredible*!"

Marcus wandered home in something of a daze, only to find that his parents had gone out.

"I've had to stay in because of you," grumbled his elder sister, Emily.

"Why?"

"Because you were out, stupid, that's why," she told him, returning her attention to the magazine she was reading. "Now feed the cat to save me a job."

Marcus pulled a face at her and then trailed into the kitchen.

"Jinks!" he called out, rattling the cat's bowl. "C'mon, Jinks – teatime."

As if by magic, Jinks appeared at his side. Only the tinkle of the cat flap in the kitchen door gave away her entrance. Jinks began to rub herself up against his jeans, purring, while Marcus emptied a tin of meat into the bowl.

Marcus teased the cat by pretending to put the bowl down on the floor, only to whip it away as soon as Jinks tried to start eating. When he did this for the third time, Jinks flicked out her paw and scratched the back of his hand.

"Ouch!" he winced, dropping the bowl.

As Jinks tucked into her food, Marcus examined the red scratches and wiped away a smear of blood.

"Right, cat, you've had it now," he warned.

He skimmed through the pages of his sketchbook and found one of the pictures of Jinks – then took the rubber out of his pocket ...

At School

... where Marcus has one of those days when everything seems to go wrong, but it's even worse for other people who cross him ...

"Have you seen Jinks this morning, Marcus?" asked his mum.

He put his spoon into the empty cereal bowl and got up from the breakfast table to sort out his bag for school. He slipped his sketchbook in last and made sure that the rubber was tucked away beneath his PE kit. He couldn't risk leaving it lying around anywhere at home.

"Well? Have you?" Mum repeated.

He shook his head, trying to look busy rather than guilty.

"She didn't even finish her meal yesterday," Mum said. "Do you know why?"

Marcus gave a shrug. "She just disappeared," he said, slinging the bag over his shoulder. "Sorry, got to go – I'm a bit late."

"Don't worry, Mum. I'm sure she'll turn up soon," said Emily as the back door slammed shut.

Morning school was taken up mostly by number work and writing, with a break for PE in between. For some children, this was the best part of Monday, but not for Marcus. For him, that was still to come – the art and craft session after lunch.

As usual, he was the last one to finish changing for PE and the last to arrive in the hall. Most of the apparatus had already been set up.

"Put the flags out," sneered Tom. "Sticky's finally made it."

Tom was always inventing nicknames for people, but his mate Aziz, otherwise known as Zed because of the two 'z's in his name, was puzzled by this one.

"Why Sticky?" he asked.

"Well – just look at his legs. They're as thin as a stick insect's!"

Even the teacher, Mr Fisher – *Fishface* to Tom this week – greeted Marcus in a sarcastic tone.

"Welcome, Marcus. It's nice of you to join us," he said. "Help Tom and Aziz put the mats out, please, and then start to warm up."

"Huh!" Tom grunted, not pleased. "You just keep out of our way, Sticky."

"Yeah!" Aziz agreed. "You might bump into us and snap off one of your legs!"

The PE lesson did not go well for the clumsy Marcus, who found himself in a tangle on a piece of climbing apparatus.

"Look, Zed – Sticky's got stuck!" Tom cackled.

Aziz helped Marcus down only by pushing him off, and he landed heavily on the thick crash mat below.

"Uuff!" gasped Marcus as all the breath was forced out of his body.

Marcus decided to seek his revenge at lunchtime. He sat by a hedge on the playing field near to where Tom and Aziz were kicking a ball about, and began to draw cartoon-style versions of them.

Their faces would have been recognised by anyone, but he gave them both animal bodies in football kits. The podgy Tom was made to look like a hippopotamus with a bulging shirt, while the long-necked, long-legged Aziz was turned into a giraffe.

Marcus chuckled to himself as he worked, pleased with his comical sketches. He might have been happy to leave it at that, close the book and walk away, but before he could do so, Tom spotted him.

"Hey! What are you doing there, Sticky?" he shouted.

"He's got that sketchbook of his," said Aziz. "He's always drawing something."

"Well he'd better not be drawing us," Tom muttered. "C'mon, Zed, let's go and check it out."

Marcus saw the pair heading towards him and panicked. There was no way he could let them see the pictures. They'd kill him!

He decided to act first – and fast. Grabbing the rubber, Marcus used it so vigorously that he even made a hole in the paper in wiping it clean ...

In the Classroom

... where Marcus enjoys the afternoon art and craft session until somebody else takes a fancy to his rubber ...

"Does anyone know where Tom and Aziz have got to?"

Mr Fisher looked up from the register to see a lot of shaking heads. One girl then put up her hand.

"I saw them playing football just before the bell went, Mr Fisher," she said, "but when I looked again, they'd disappeared."

The teacher sent two boys off on a fruitless search, and began to organise the classroom for various craft activities. Marcus had already chosen to paint – as usual – and was given the job of organising the materials that his group needed.

"And make sure you clean the brushes properly afterwards," Mr Fisher told him. "You left them in the sink last time still covered in paint, remember."

Marcus remembered. He'd had to stay in at break the next morning to clean every brush the teacher could find – and then to clean the sink itself.

35

Mr Fisher wanted the children to explore the theme of symmetry, and Marcus decided to use his rubber as a model. Not only was its diamond shape symmetrical, but so were the jagged markings on its surfaces.

Marcus put the rubber on the table in front of him and began to outline its patterns on his paper.

"Nice rubber, Marcus," said the girl next to him. "Where did you get it?"

"Market," he grunted, trying to concentrate.

"Thought so."

Marcus looked at her. "How d'yer mean – *thought so*?"

Chloe smirked. "Because I saw it there as well."

He gave a shrug. "So?"

"And I also saw what you did," she hissed.

Marcus made no effort to deny the theft and carried on with his painting. He was using bright red for the teeth-like markings.

"So *I* want it now," Chloe added. "Give it to me."

He shook his head. "It's mine."

Chloe's response came straight back.

"If you don't let me have it, I'll tell Mr Fisher what happened yesterday."

"No you won't."

"You can't stop me."

Marcus picked up the rubber. "Oh yes, I can," he said.

"And you can't stop me doing this, either," Chloe replied.

Chloe reached out and knocked over a tub of dirty water so that it spilled right across his painting, making all the colours run like blood. Before Marcus could react, Mr Fisher walked by.

"That was very careless, Marcus," said the teacher sternly. "You'll have to clean up that mess and start again."

Marcus was furious – with both of them. He went to fetch a cloth from the sink to wipe the table and then took another piece of paper into the book corner, well away from everybody. He didn't need any paints. A pencil would be enough for what he intended to draw now – and the rubber of course.

Two faces soon began to take shape beneath his skilful fingers ...

"What are you doing down there, Marcus?"

Marcus looked up at Mr Fisher from the carpet. "Just drawing," he replied.

"Let me see."

He reluctantly handed the paper to the teacher, who stared at the pictures and then back at Marcus.

"Why draw me and Chloe?" asked Mr Fisher. "We're not exactly symmetrical."

Marcus reddened slightly. "Got bored with symmetry," he mumbled.

"Bored, eh? Well, then, we'd better find you something to do. How about cleaning some more brushes? You're good at that."

Back Home

... where Marcus decides that enough is enough, but can he pluck up the courage to end it? ...

Marcus arrived back home in a bad mood, disturbing his sister, who was trying to revise for college exams. Emily complained to their mum, and Marcus made matters worse by being rude to her too. He was sent up to his bedroom out of the way until teatime.

He took the sketchbook out of his school bag and lay on the bed, doodling, the rubber by his side. Without quite realising what he was doing, a face began to appear beneath his pencil. He was shocked at first to see who it was, but still carried on until he had finished the picture of Emily.

When he reached for the rubber, however, he felt as if he was going to be sick. He sat up to let the sensation pass.

"I can't keep doing this," he murmured. "But how can I stop it?"

Marcus turned to the page where he had sketched the rubber itself and started to draw another face next to it – his own.

"Perhaps it's the only way," he said, shaking his head sadly.

He heaved a sigh and picked up the rubber for the last time.

As it went to work, the glistening red patterns began to fade ...

"Marcus?"

When there was no reply, Mum came up the stairs. "Come on, Marcus, your tea's on the table," she said from outside his room. "There's no need to sulk."

She pushed open the door to find the room empty, his sketchbook lying neglected on the floor.

As she picked up the sketchbook to admire his portrait, Marcus popped up behind her.

"Sorry, Mum. Did you call?" he asked.

"You know I did. Where were you?"

"In the bathroom," he told her. "I was just washing off some red paint stains, ready for tea."

Marcus held out his hands to prove they were clean.

"All gone, look," he said, grinning.

So was the rubber.

Marcus had used it to erase the picture of itself from the sketchbook. The paper beside his self-portrait was now blank.

Meeeowww ...

A long wail startled them and they turned to see a cat at the top of the stairs.

"Jinks!" Mum cried, lifting her up for a cuddle. "You've come back. Where *have* you been?"

Jinks could not answer that – and neither could Marcus.

"That must mean Tom and Aziz are back too," he breathed in relief. "And the old woman. Guess I'd better keep well away from the market in future!"